MEMORABILIA

A WORK OF FACTION... FACTS BLENDED WITH FICTION.

"There is a divinity that shapes our ends,
rough-hew them how we will".
Hamlet..by William Shakespeare

GLORIA ALBERTS PRABAL

BLUEROSE PUBLISHERS
India | U.K.

Copyright © Gloria Alberts Prabal 2024

All rights reserved by author. No part of this publication may be reproduced, stored in a retrieval system or transmitted in any form or by any means, electronic, mechanical, photocopying, recording or otherwise, without the prior permission of the author. Although every precaution has been taken to verify the accuracy of the information contained herein, the publisher assume no responsibility for any errors or omissions. No liability is assumed for damages that may result from the use of information contained within.

BlueRose Publishers takes no responsibility for any damages, losses, or liabilities that may arise from the use or misuse of the information, products, or services provided in this publication.

For permissions requests or inquiries regarding this publication, please contact:

BLUEROSE PUBLISHERS
www.BlueRoseONE.com
info@bluerosepublishers.com
+91 8882 898 898
+4407342408967

ISBN: 978-93-5819-934-5

Cover design: Tahira
Typesetting: Tanya Raj Upadhyay

First Edition: June 2024

Table of Contents

Teacher's Pet 1

Shakespeare Revisited 13

Retribution 22

Hero - Reel and Real.. 35

Closure 47

Teacher's Pet

Veena Teacher was perplexed. She knit her brows in deep concentration and scrutinized the answer script for the umpteenth time: a perfect paper, not a comma or full stop out of place, no errors at all. It was really baffling. Sanjeev was not the brightest student, and he seldom crossed the forty mark. Now he scored an unprecedented eighty percent. Even her star pupil, Ranjan, was lagging behind with the normal sixty-five.

"A penny for your thoughts? Hey Veena, you look so perturbed. What's the matter, dear?" Mrs. Sandra Peters, her loquacious, inquisitive but well-meaning co-worker asked, generally concerned.

"Oh, it is nothing important, Sandy. By the way, who scored the highest in English in your section?" Veena asked casually so as not to arouse any suspicion.

"The paper was pretty tough this time, so my boy Vikram just managed a sixty. I had a couple of failures too. What about your class?" Sandy asked.

"Well, a dark horse, Sanjeev managed to edge past the regular toppers and secure a whopping eighty."

Veena paused; she wanted to see Sandy's reaction. But Mrs. Sandra Peters seemed pleased that at least one student did well. The Chairman of the Academic Council will grill teachers if he finds anomalies. Too many high scores were bad news, as were too many failures.

"That is okay, Veena. He has done well. Come on, have your coffee. In any case, what is your problem? Do not trouble trouble until trouble troubles you!" she laughed out loud enough to make heads turn in the staff room. Veena and Sandy shared a good rapport, which was the envy of their colleagues. However, today Veena was in no mood to smell the coffee. A lot of negative thoughts assailed Veena. Did Sanjeev go for tuition to the wily Mansi Prasad? She had heard that Simon Raj also had a coaching center.

"Had your coffee, Simon?" Veena asked chattily. "How did your kids fare in your language test?" Simon was taciturn and grave, devoid of a sense of humor but in the classroom, he was a genius.

"The usual, can't remember who scored the highest. I think it was Neeraj with fifty-eight." Now Veena was visibly rattled. She had to tread cautiously to tackle her third co-worker. Manasi Prasad's father-in-law was the District Judge, and Manasi let it be known to all that Papaji was the best legal luminary in the state and had the power to "hang people by neck until death." Her husband Samir was into real estate, and both her boys were in "Doon." Manasi was very status conscious and cocked a snook at other teachers, so Veena was on a sticky wicket.

"Manasi, I'll be shopping in M.G. Road today. If I finish my work, I may drop in around seven?"

Manasi was effusive and warm.

"Yes, that would be nice, Veena, do join us for dinner, I'll drop you back."

Veena was overwhelmed with happiness but declined the offer for dinner. That evening, Veena had finished her work earlier than expected and made her way towards Judge Prasad's house.

On reaching the gate, as soon as Veena opened the gate, the security guards stood to attention and questioned her. But she stood frozen on her tracks. There was a bunch of students who were equally taken aback to see Veena Teacher, and there stood the red-faced Manasi, clearly embarrassed at being caught red-handed with so many students who had, no doubt, come for tuition. So, this was her additional source of income! The students hastily darted off, and Veena slowly walked towards Manasi Prasad, who smiled sheepishly.

"Come in, Veena," she said weakly and ordered coffee and a platter of assorted biscuits for Veena.

She just made some small talk to justify her visit.

"I was up to my neck with corrections, just needed a break. English language corrections are the worst, so tedious, and time-consuming. Who scored the highest?" she asked innocuously.

"I can't remember," Manasi said, clearly ill at ease. Veena thanked Manasi for the coffee and left. She drew a blank; it was an exercise in futility.

There was clearly something very fishy about Sanjeev's marks. It's best to inform the principal. The eagle-eyed Mr. Henderson, would be quick to spot the disparity in the marks given in one section, and then there will be "hell to smell," his favorite phrase. Veena had two consecutive free periods and decided to settle this matter before the Boss.

Mr. Dennis Henderson bore a striking resemblance to the legendary Bob Dylan. The senior teachers often wondered why he did not comb his hair but the outgoing students found the reclusive bachelor very endearing and even regarded him as a trend-setter. They conferred on him the moniker "Trendy Hendy" in private, and he, in turn, quite reveled in this show of affection.

But beneath his "carefully careless" exterior, he was a strict disciplinarian who brooked no nonsense from staff or students. Veena had mentally prepared an elaborate account of what to say, but when she sat opposite Mr. Henderson, she faltered as if she was the villain of the piece.

"Yes, Mrs. Shekher?" Mr. Henderson did not waste time and let it be known.

"Sir, it is regarding my class XII science student Sanjeev ...." She completed the story in one long-winded sentence that left her and the shmoozed Principal breathless.

"So, you suspect there is more to it than what meets the eye?"

"Yes, Sir."

"Okay, let's hear the young lad's version, and punishment will be awarded accordingly. The law of natural justice, you know. I would like to meet Sanjeev, his parents, and you tomorrow at 11:30 sharp. This is to be kept strictly confidential. Thank you."

The next day Mr. and Mrs. Bhagat waited in the parlor seriously wondering what their obedient and god-fearing son had done. On questioning him, Sanjeev told his parents it was regarding some signatures. His simple, gullible parents were more than happy to affix signatures. But now they realized to their dismay, that they were the only parents present in the parlor. Panic struck when they saw Mr. Henderson enter his office along with three teachers and Sanjeev! Exactly at 11:30 AM, the Bhagat's were inside the principal's spacious but unkempt office.

After they were all seated, except Sanjeev, Mr. Henderson wished them all politely but gravely.

"Now Sanjeev, just tell us how you happened to do so well in your language examination."

Sanjeev's parents looked at each other in shock and disbelief. The other three teachers looked uncomfortable. What was happening, only Veena and Henderson seemed to be privy to the matter.

Sanjeev also came straight to the point, "Sir, I knew what was coming." He blurted out. Simon looked at his fingertips and carefully examined them to avoid direct eye contact. Manasi kept adjusting the folds of her silk saree. Sandy looked open-mouthed, "Oh my gosh, really?"

Veena prayed fervently that the culprit should be severely taken to task. She seethed with rage at the tuition teachers who ran parallel schools.

"So, my boy, you can tell us your side of the story." The principal, a superb administrator, knew how to put everyone at ease, and he ordered some tea and snacks while a nice story was unfolding.

"Sir, my Exams were on Monday. No Sir, Tuesday. Monday was Janam astami, a holiday. On Saturday it was Daljit's birthday. He had invited us to a party and said sharp six the cake would be cut. Sir, I had to do some chores for my mother, so I got late...." Sanjeev paused and looked towards his parents and then towards Veena, "Go on son" said the principal in his trademark soft voice that normally spelt trouble. Simon thought: "This looks like a page from a Who Dunnit novel, so exciting, and intriguing." Then, after an interminably long silence, Sanjeev continued.

"Sir, then I decided to take a short cut and I jumped over the wall into the school yard. I saw guard Uncle coming towards me, so I crouched inside the pit."

"The pit?" they all asked, clearly mesmerized by this seventeen-year old's adventure.

"Yes, Sir, the pit. I could see many papers burning, the smoke was getting into my eyes, but I could make out these were question papers. I poked the rubble with a stick, one paper was clear. It was the class XII English language paper. I shoved it into my pocket and ran before the guard could see me." He stopped.

"Only one question paper?" The principal questioned sardonically.

"No, Sir, there were many papers, but all were burnt and... sorry Sir." Sanjeev's father sprang up like a wounded tiger and slapped him hard across the face. Even the unflappable Mr. Henderson was caught unawares.

"You damn rascal, you come home, and I'll show you."

Mrs. Bhagat took out her small floral handkerchief from her handbag and kept wiping her tears.

"Sir Henderson, I am apologizing on behalf of my son. Please punish him Sir, but don't give TC please Sir." Mr. Henderson's impassive face added to the Bhagats' woes. There was palpable silence, and all four teachers were relieved that somehow, they were not involved in this heinous crime. All waited with bated breaths to see what Mr. Henderson would do. He scribbled something in his notepad and after what seemed like eternity, he spoke in a measured tone.

"I have made a note of the case. I shall inform you about the quantum of punishment at 2:30. I've arranged for some refreshments in the parlor. Please help yourselves."

"Oh no," groaned Mr. Simon as soon as Boss left the room. It was Mr. Simon's duty to pick up the children from school.

"Justice delayed is justice denied," Manasi added unnecessarily. "I wonder what's up his sleeves?"

Veena was clearly upset with this story: the actual wrongdoers would go scot-free.

The meeting was reconvened exactly at 2:30. The somber mood returned post-lunch, and all took their respective seats, save Sanjeev, who was asked to wait outside. "This is no doubt a matter of grave concern and necessitates exemplary punishment. However, I had kept three things in mind as I deliberated and mulled over this issue." Mr. Henderson lowered his voice to create suspense. "Firstly, Sanjeev is a class twelve student, and any stringent punishment on the eve of his examination will be detrimental to the student and the school. It may even jeopardize his future. Secondly, Sanjeev did not exactly cheat. He fell into a pit, stumbled upon some burning papers, which happened to be question papers, picked up what he thought was his language paper—not a crime, in my opinion. However, since he jumped into the school premises unauthorized, he will be suspended for two days, as per our school policy. Anyone here has something to say?" He knew his verdict was final, but he asked each one individually.

"Mr. Bhagat?"

"Mrs. Bhagat, Madam?"

All looked down "Okay, so the matter is settled. Parents, please collect the suspension letter before you go home."

Mr. Bhagat ran towards Mr. Henderson and touched his feet and kept mumbling "Thank you, Sir" multiple times.

It was a diktat from the Boss that what was discussed within closed doors in the office was never to be discussed in the staff room.

Sanjeev served his suspension and joined school on Monday and nonchalantly went about his business.

Thus, he was taken aback when, on the following day the peon handed a note to his class teacher, Veena. The principal wanted to see Sanjeev.

"Yes, Sir. Good morning, Sir."

Mr. Henderson looked Sanjeev straight in the eye and said, "Now tell me the truth, the whole truth and nothing but the truth."

"Sir, I found the question paper lying on the floor, in my classroom. Mrs. Veena had left her bag on the table. I had gone back to take my Tiffin box. I knew Veena Teacher had gone down to the staff room. So, I read and memorized the composition, the report, and some grammar portions."

The principal nodded. Apparently, he knew all along because he was very meticulous and thorough in his investigation. He knew that Sanjeev was lying through his teeth. So, he cross-checked with all the supporting staff and another picture emerged.

"But why did you concoct such a bizarre story?" Mr. Henderson was clearly intrigued by this.

"Sir, I did not want Veena Teacher to get into trouble."

Shakespeare Revisited

"Glory teacher, do you know what happened during our trip to Kolkata?" The precocious Milesh was bursting at the seams with excitement and could scarcely suppress his giggles. Glory teacher put down her "Merchant of Venice" textbook to listen to the National Broadcasting Corporation's version of what happened.

NBC nicknamed Nilesh Broadcasting Corporation always came up with some nuggets of juicy information, mostly harmless tidbits of events in the neighborhood. Sometimes, he would wax eloquent on the Iraq-Iran War, and sometimes, he would discuss random friends' quirks.

Glory Banerjee, popularly called Glory B by friends and colleagues, feigned this interest, but closing her textbook was a sure-shot indication of her eagerness to know what had happened. The outgoing batch of tenth graders was normally treated to a picnic or excursion on the outskirts of the Steel City.

However, this year, the principal, in a rare display of magnanimity, informed the class that they would be going to Kolkata. 'Kolkata' the euphoria was expected and soon all thirty students' parents signed up the approval form without batting an eyelid. Three teachers were to accompany the students, Mrs. Lily Sen, the class teacher - who also taught mathematics, was not too keen on going because of the impending Puja season.

But it was mandatory for the class teacher to accompany these "Super-brats" as the tenth graders loved to call themselves. Mrs. Baker, who loved 'Cal' and enjoyed the "Kati rolls and dal purees" was now reluctant to go due to severe arthritis. However, Deep Ranjan Mishra, the Games teacher, was game literally, and looked forward to this trip. The students discussed the trio during recess the day their names were announced.

"Why must Miss Pythagoras come with us? She is so strict," one grumbled. "Yes, I'm sure she will make us do all the calculations, measure the platform, the speed of the train and profit and loss." The students quite loved Mrs. Baker who, true to her name, controlled the Cookery Department, and since only a few students had opted for cookery, nobody was scared of her. She passed muster and they even joked wittily, "better Mrs. Baker than Mrs. Shekhar (the Physics Teacher)."

But all thirty were unanimous in the high rating for Mr. DRM "no fear, all fun," they wholeheartedly approved of him. The students were no doubt apprehensive about Miss Lily's presence. They memorized all the theorems, formulas, all the names of angles and triangles. It looked like the students were preparing for the math's Olympiad rather than a fun filled excursion.

Lily Sen had the happy knack of springing a surprise on the students' parents and guardians. She would lambaste the parents and plait her scanty hair simultaneously. It was rumored that even the principal avoided a direct confrontation with Lily Sen! Like all teachers, past, present and to come, Miss Lily also was susceptible to flattery.

The senior students would mill around her and as if on cue, one would say "Miss your saree is so beautiful" and then add, "Miss, will we get theorems in the exam?" The students tried their best to elicit some hints, but like all teachers, she reveled in the adulation but was tightlipped regarding the questions.

In spite of her quirks, howlers and mannerisms, students adored her and parents felt their children would be kept on the tight leash by Miss Sen and of course Mrs. Baker would add the motherly touch and Sir DRM would provide the much-needed respite from studies.

The itinerary for the two days trip was meticulously chalked out, a visit to the museum Nicco Park, Birla Planetarium and Victoria Memorial. There were also places of entertainment, shopping and food. The class of thirty enjoyed themselves to the hilt, savoring the street food, buying little baubles and trinkets, gaping at the humongous multitudes on the street, the gigantic hoarding, the trams, the rickshaws, Park Street and Eden Gardens.

On the second day, at 2 PM, the students were taken to Victoria Memorial with their knapsacks. This bunch of teenagers was not very interested in the history of Victoria Memorial. They preferred to be in the open space and engage in idle banter.

Mrs. Baker wielded the cane, which served a dual purpose, a walking stick and keeping the flock together. Despite their best efforts, the students began to wander about aimlessly in groups and Mrs. Baker's high-pitched voice could be heard "Hide where I can see you," that is exactly what the high-spirited class did not do. Mrs. Baker evoked no dread, no fear, but immense love and goodwill.

She was the most senior teacher in the school, having served with unstinting loyalty and devotion for over three decades. Taking into consideration her exemplary track record and keeping in mind her superannuation the following year, the Board unanimously agreed to elevate her to the post of senior coordinator. Subsequently, she was an integral part of all events in the senior section, becoming a confidante and agony aunt to teachers and students alike.

Mrs. Lily Sen was relieved when she spotted Mrs. Baker with her walking stick and Mr. DRM with his whistle hovering around the students. She ambled slowly towards the gate where the spicy, tangy, tantalizing pucchkas beckoned her.

"Five rupees for ten," the scruffy Pucchkawala said. "No, no twelve, dada." He nodded, wiped his grimy hands on his dhoti, which had not seen any soap of any description and then got down to work. It was heavenly, all the ideas of hygiene vanished as she held the cracked orb, stuffed with pungent 'filling', opened her mouth wide and almost choked. Then she popped another and another. It was sheer bliss, she closed her eyes, oblivious to the world around her.

Then disaster struck! She howled in excruciating agony as she tried to yank the offending bee that had stung her on her left ear lobe. In doing so, she pulled the earring out and flung it, literally throwing the baby with (not in) the bath water!! Now, even as she was writhing in pain, she became conscious of the fact that her diamond earring was missing.

"Oh my god, my earring, oh my god " she wailed loud enough to bring the buying and selling of Puchkas and Jhalmuri to a standstill. "What happened Masi Ma (aunt)?. Don't cry, everything will be alright." This inane sentence was bad enough; what was worse was the curious onlookers asking her *ad nauseum*, "But where did it fall?"

The Pucchkawala was a trifle annoyed because she had eaten five pucchkas and not paid a penny. Now he added to the confusion by shouting at her. The motley crowd that gathered soon disappeared, though some urchins and loiterers were seen digging in the hope of finding the earring.

Mrs. Baker was wondering why Miss Lily was on her fours, peering into the grassy patch. She informed DRM and soon the entire class was at her side, commiserating with her. "Miss, please sit down, we will look for your earring. Don't cry, Miss". Someone offered her a glass of water. In between sips of water, sobs and blowing of the nose, she narrated the misfortune that had befallen her.

"Yes, a bee stung me on my earlobe, and I inadvertently threw my earring." The students were sad. Mrs. Baker, a devout Catholic and a devotee of Saint Anthony, quietly offered some prayers to the Saint. Mr. Mishra applied some cream to Miss Lily's earlobe. Now it was time to leave. The Howrah Steel City Super-Fast Express would leave at 5:30 PM and so the students had to get a bus or cab to Howrah Station at the earliest.

Miss Lily Sen just could not fathom what to do. How could she leave without her earring, a diamond and a priceless piece of jewelry? But the barrage of questions from her students unnerved and exhausted her and it was time to leave the sprawling, lush green fields with her earring embedded somewhere—a tragedy of gigantic proportion.

"Mr. Mishra, please proceed towards the station in batches. Come children stay close together," she said weakly. "Mrs. Baker please take the roll call; we don't want any more disasters." "Hey where is Rizwan? Did anyone see him? Mr. Mishra, please blow your whistle. Oh my god, what is happening today?" Miss Lily was now almost hysterical.

Now there was another pandemonium and finally someone spotted him near the Pucchka stall. "Now what on earth is he doing there, that rascal," Mr. Mishra said, exasperated by the dramatic turn of events. "I am going to give him a nice whack." Mr. Mishra's face was distorted with impotent rage; corporal punishment was not allowed. "Come here, you naughty boy." Rizwan came panting towards the group, fist tight.

"Miss your earring" Rizwan whispered. There was pin drop, silence. Miss Lily's face lit up like a million stars, like a bright Christmas Tree. "How, my boy, how?". She could hardly speak. Rizwan smiled and said slowly "Miss it's a long story." "What story"? They queried in unison.

In "Miss, in the Merchant of Venice," a play by Shakespeare, Bassanio threw a dart to recover the lost dart. I applied the same principle, and I retrieved your earring." No one believed the story but, as they say, all is well that ends well.

When the excitement of the earring and excursion abated, Miss Lily asked Rizwan how he could retrieve the lost earring when she hadn't given him the other odd. "It just doesn't add up," she said. The pun was not lost on Rizwan. He smiled broadly and said, "Miss, I was the last boy to go for pucckhas. The puccha seller was grumbling about some money you owed him. So, I paid the money, and in return, he handed me a stone - your diamond earring!!"

Retribution

Jeet Bahadur Rana allowed himself the luxury of an A.C. compartment: a first-class coupe, no less. He adjusted his belongings, and although it was a tad cold inside, he ensconced himself comfortably on the upper berth. His Bengali co-passengers were chatting merrily, nineteen to the dozen, about some forthcoming elections. The atmosphere was charged with high decibel, high-tensile debates about who should, could, would win, and why.

Jeet Bahadur Rana, as he was popularly known, thanked his lucky stars that he had bought a couple of sports magazines. Though eager to add his own two pennies to the conversation, he decided against it. He propped himself on his makeshift pillow and started flipping through the pages of his second-hand magazine. Bengalis are passionate about both sports and politics, and soon they borrowed his magazines and offered him some nice home-cooked food.

Exactly at 8 PM, the Howrah Patliputra Express lurched forward and started moving like a gigantic caterpillar. Soon, the train gained momentum, and the bone-rattling caterpillar compelled everyone to quieten down.

Jeet Bahadur Rana stared vacantly at the glossy sports star which featured the great Sunil Gavaskar on the cover. He rued the opportunities missed. He was a budding sportsperson himself. His father, a cobbler, toiled by the sweat of his brow to give his children a decent education, but Jeet was not inclined to anything even remotely academic. He pinned his hopes and aspirations on football. He was barely sixteen when a devastating earthquake ravaged his small hamlet near Biratnagar. Nothing much could be salvaged from the debris, but he was grateful his family survived. The earthquake brought death, destruction, and destitution. The Ranas sold their land, gave each of his grown-up sons their share, and sought refuge in an ashram.

Jeet, a tall strapping lad, had boarded a bus to Patna armed with his class X certificates, sports trophies, and medals. He secured his money between his clothes; the money had to stretch until he found himself a decent job. When he reached Patna, fear gripped him. Nobody seemed overly interested in hiring a Nepali boy with a sob story. During the day, he roamed around hoping somebody would give him a square meal. One cold wintery morning, he swooned. And thus, Jeet, the ace goalkeeper in his school, lay unconscious on the footpath of a nondescript lane in Patna.

When he regained consciousness, he was terror-stricken. Where was he? He had heard horror stories of human trafficking, kidnapping, mutilating, by unscrupulous avaricious men, mainly drug peddlers. Was he a victim of this racket? Just as he was in deep contemplation, a kindly benign figure attired in white entered his little room. He introduced himself as Father Anthony and offered the bewildered Jeet a glass of lime juice, which he gulped down gratefully.

"Feeling better now, beta?" Jeet was a bit skeptical at first, being a devout Hindu, he had never interacted with men of other faith.

"Yes, Sir, thank you. Sir, I want to go home Biratnagar, Nepal." He cried, and Father Anthony patted the boy's shoulders and said, "Tell me about your family, and I'll see what I can do." That was the beginning of a long-lasting friendship between a teenager from Nepal and a septuagenarian from Portugal. Both came to his great land for two diametrically opposite quests: one for spiritual and the other for material. Both shared a deep love for football and cinema.

Fr. Anthony told Jeet about a school adjacent to the church. He could work there as a physical education teacher, and also coach the boys in football. Father's recommendation letter carried weight, and so Jeet landed his first job by the time he was eighteen. The geriatric Christian Priest and the young sprightly Nepali lad soon became inseparable.

"Your biological father and your spiritual father are both menders of souls/soles," he would joke along the way, teaching him conversational English which would stand him in good stead in the years to come. He was now on firm footing. After a decade or so, Father Anthony left for his heavenly abode – but he left Jeet with a great legacy, a deep abiding faith in his religion, and an all-encompassing love for humanity. Jeet wept inconsolably for days and decided to leave Patna.

"Boy, the show must go on," he could hear Father say, and Jeet moved to greener pastures. He reached Calcutta armed with a string of degrees and testimonials. He responded to advertisements in the newspaper and was now employed as a teacher at the prestigious Calcutta International Academy – a school exclusively for the elite.

"Welcome to the CALINA family, Mr. Jeet Bahadur Rana," the Principal, Mr. Rangarajan, warmly welcomed him. He was in charge of the Junior section, and there he met his future wife Meena, a helper teacher. After a couple of months of courtship, they decided to tie the knot in a low-key ceremony in the local temple. His ailing parents and good-for-nothing siblings regretted their inability to attend but sent him long letters filled with manifold blessings. Rohit even slyly asked what he received by way of dowry.

"See Bhaiya, you are working as a master in an English-medium school, so I hope you are getting a good amount in cash. Mother is sick, you know, and money is..."

Jeet slammed the phone in the PCO. He and Meena emptied their coffers to buy important household appliances and simple furniture.

Three children were born within eight years span, and his financial liabilities increased. His parents had since passed away, but his siblings kept asking for help one way or another.

Ritu, his eldest sister, was perpetually crying poverty and would not miss an opportunity to prey on his sentiments.

"You know, when you were small, I always gave you my share of guava..."

"When you were sick, I gave you..." the list of things she purportedly gave Jeet was never-ending. But now he had to put his foot down. Radhika, his eldest daughter, was an exceptionally bright girl. He decided to approach the new Principal, Mr. Varghese.

"Sir, please, if you could kindly waive Radhika's fees. I have brought her report cards, Sir. She comes first in class."

Mr. Varghese weighed the consequences and after an interminably long silence said, "Okay, Mr. Rana, I will strongly recommend your case before the managing committee on compassionate grounds. However, if you want to buttress your case, I suggest you volunteer to teach the boys cricket after school. Then I am pretty sure you'll get more concessions." Mr. Varghese knew how to extract work from the teachers.

"Yes, Sir, I'll start coaching the boys from tomorrow." He was willing to walk that extra mile if it helped Radhika. Jeet was making a name for himself as a great sports and games master, and he was getting lucrative offers from rival schools. But he was loyal to the institution, where his whole family was beholden to the school and the management.

"Don't be so naive, Jeetu, look at the perks in a government school, no accountability. Here, if you lose one ball, you are answerable to everyone," his friends taunted him. Jeet was tempted to go to those schools, which had total job security. No doubt he weighed the pros and cons. His salary was not too bad. Meena's income augmented his resources.

"God has blessed me immensely. I do not need to move." He was a happy man. The high watermark in his career was when the fledgling cricket team won the championship trophy for three consecutive years. This hat trick pitched Jeet to the pinnacle of fame and glory. The Board, in recognition of his perseverance, dedication, and loyalty, honored him with the Best Teacher award and a plaque.

In his speech before the august gathering, he briefly outlined his sojourn from a tiny shanty in Nepal to a prestigious school in a metropolis. The standing ovation he received was proof of his popularity and passion for sports. As a gesture of thanksgiving, he offered prayers in the temple and fed the destitute and needy in the vicinity.

Radhika scored an impressive ninety percent on her Boards; there was much jubilation in Rana's house. She was their joy and pride. The two boys were least interested in studies, but Vikram followed in his father's footsteps and excelled in sports, while the youngest Ranjit was a budding artist.

"Papa, I want to take up arts," said Radhika, the Ranas were disappointed. They had wanted Radhika to go into Engineering or Medicine.

The principal supported his star pupil's decision to opt for Arts. Radha explained to her parents that she wanted to join the civil service. Moreover, science students ran from pillar to post for tuition, but she wanted free time to write, read, and participate in curricular activities. Radhika was a prolific writer and an ace debater, and so her parents were pacified.

Then trouble started: Rupesh Kumar Das was tipped off by the friendly secretary about his son's name being second to Radhika's. Preetam was a happy-go-lucky plodder who treated his friends to lavish meals in fancy restaurants, so they voted for him en mass. The staff too, were recipients of largesse from the Das family.

"This is a small gift for taking care of my son." The small gift was invariably a gold ring! So many teachers found this inheritor an apt candidate to represent the school!

But Rupesh Kumar was in a pensive mood today. The crucial board meeting was scheduled for Friday. That his son was pipped at the post by a mere teacher's daughter was a slight he could not digest. He had to work out a strategy.

His wife, heavily decked in silk and gold, offered him unsolicited advice. "See, everyone is for sale; offer him some money, and he will make Radhika withdraw the nomination."

"I can't do that. I am a Board Member," Rupesh vetoed this ridiculous idea. He could not bribe the upright Ranas. Their integrity was unquestionable.

Rupesh was a manipulator, a wheeler-dealer, and he knew how to hone his way. He read the selection/elimination criteria again and again. The school constitution suddenly became his newfound holy book. He was once told this by his business friend.

"There are two ways to attack your enemy: One is to directly slay him with your Talwar, the other is to use one simple safety pin and keep pricking him every now and then." He decided on the pinprick.

As Vice Chairman, he was vested with enormous powers: academics, finance and building. All came within his jurisdiction.

On Monday, he summoned Mr. Rana to his office about five kilometers from the school. "Look here, Mr. Rana, I have noticed that you have broken many school rules."

"No, Sir, I have been working in this institution for over twenty years." Jeet Bahadur Rana was shocked and hurt by these unfounded allegations.

"Your wife is working here, your daughter is availing a hefty concession; your two sons are showing no progress in academics. You know ours is a much sought-after school. If your sons find it difficult to cope, please let them go to some vernacular medium school." Jeet Rana was shell-shocked. But the pinpricks had just started.

"And yes, the reason I brought this matter up today is because I received a couple of letters signed by parents sayings that your daughter Radhika has been bunking school multiple times. Clearly, Rana, your family is taking full advantage of the school. I'm afraid I have to place this before the managing committee."

Mr. Rana shrank in his chair all of a sudden, and so many points were raised against him. He had nothing to say in his defense. Radhika was caught red-handed bunking. He felt so betrayed. Tears welled up in his eyes. Rupesh looked sympathetically at Jeet Bahadur Rana. "I can help you tide over this crisis."

"Okay Sir, thank you. So kind of you Sir. Please forgive Radhika. I'll punish her for this." Jeet cried in pain and humiliation.

"No, no, don't tell her anything; girls are very sensitive at this age. She'll do something drastic, then you will never forgive yourself."

"Mr. Rana, just keep this discussion strictly confidential. When Radhika's name is announced in the assembly for the International Exchange Program, just write a letter stating she suffers from migraine or any such ailment and hence you wish to withdraw her nomination. Let the Principal and Board decide."

Jeet Bahadur did not quite comprehend the whole matter, and he agreed instantly. The grateful Mr. Rana quickly made his exit, oblivious to the trap he fell into.

A week later, Radhika's name was announced at the Assembly as the school representative in the International Student Exchange Program. Radhika was filled with pride and happiness as the school cheered her nomination, and within one hour, Mr. Rana promptly wrote a request letter, much to Radhika's shock.

"Papa, I didn't ever bunk to drink water. Who is the writer, what is this?" she cried in dismay and disbelief.

Subsequently, Preetam Kumar Das packed his bags and flew to the U.S.A. to represent his school and country! No one even realized he was gone. It was only when Preetam Kumar returned that Jeet B. Rana asked him where he had disappeared with the sports room keys.

"Oh Sir, I went to New Jersey for the Student Exchange Program!"

Jeet Bahadur was stunned, so Rupesh Kumar Das got him to withdraw Radhika's name on the basis of trumped-up charges. How could he stoop so low? How could he be so mean to a poor aspiring student? That night, he wept bitterly, but Radhika stood by him like the Rock of Gibraltar.

"No papa, don't cry, I will bring honor and glory, I have already submitted some poems for publication." Radhika finished her class XII successfully with ninety-five percent but, unfortunately, Preetam failed. According to the School Constitution, a class XII failure was not readmitted to the school.

Ironically, at the prize distribution ceremony, Radhika Rana walked away with the much coveted – "The Rai Bahadur Gopal Chand Das Memorial AllRounder Trophy."

Mr. Jeet Bahadur Rana resigned the following month, but before doing so, he had sent his wife and children away to Delhi to start life afresh.

Meanwhile, Radhika's first Novel was published, 'Nemesis... the goddess of vengeance.'

Hero - Reel and Real

It was touted as the biggest event ever hosted in the steel city of Rampur. The star attraction was Raghav Kumar, the reigning superstar and heartthrob of the nation. His pink face and brown eyes, long black eyelashes and candy floss pink lips, painted to reveal sparkling white teeth, were plastered on the posters. Romeo Raghav, a moniker he earned due to his propensity for playing the eternal lover boy, was at the pinnacle of fame and fortune. His face and life history appeared in a plethora of film magazines, and friendly, well-pampered journalists and pen pushers lavished praise on his acting skills and even audaciously compared him to the Thespian. The rumor mill worked overtime to churn out juicy, salacious tidbits of his activities, but come Friday, the matinee idol swept everyone off their feet. Such was his star power.

Along with RK, lesser-known stars were also squeezed into the posters. All in all, apart from the supernova, a medley of stars, singers and sidekicks were part of this show.

The well-healed Ram Swaroop Agarwal, Owner and Director of Agarwal Steel Works, wanted to invest in a huge shopping complex akin to Calcutta's iconic New Market. The Ram Swaroop Super Market was designed by a renowned architect from Bengal and Rajasthan. Ram Swaroop left no stone unturned to see his dream project crystallizing. It was his son Rohit's idea to invite big film personalities and add color and glamour to the show.

"Dad, you have to spend money to make money." At first, Agarwal had predictably vetoed the idea of getting film folk. Battle lines were clearly drawn between father and son: both calculated the cost and loss incurred, and Rohit won. Mr. Agarwal grumbled to all and sundry about his son's wasteful extravagance, and all this was no doubt reported on page three of the daily tabloids.

The event would entail much fanfare and aggressive advertising. A mammoth marquee had been erected, and special enclosures were cordoned off for the VVIP guests. There were many pessimists and disgruntled people in the colony, many from the moral brigade, who clearly frowned upon RK and his ilk. And they wanted to stir up some trouble.

"Imagine what influence RK will have on our children; they will regard him as their role model, which is so terrible..." Mrs. Sarita Devi set the ball rolling at the Sindhi Sammelan. Everyone tried to outdo the other in portraying RK as the bane of society. The menfolk were more vociferous than their wives, who secretly drooled over RK. The sanctimonious Mr. Peters was breathing fire and brimstone at this great moral turpitude.

Ironically, amid all the clamor and protest to cancel the show, to shift the venue and to remove the posters, R.K. was certainly a hot potato (endorsing R.K.'s presence was tantamount to endorsing drugs and a hedonistic lifestyle); tickets were selling like hotcakes. Everybody was flocking to purchase tickets, and black marketers were having a field day.

I had just started teaching at Central High School, my alma mater. My father had passed away a year ago, so when the Principal, Miss. Carol Eton, a kind-hearted Irish Catholic Missionary, offered me the job in school, I agreed instantly.

"Thank you, Madam." I was happiness personified. My erstwhile teachers, now colleagues, welcomed me, and soon I was privy to all the personal and professional goings-on and enjoyed the camaraderie that prevailed in the staff room. My hitherto dismal life was now on a roll. We were debt-ridden, and my mother had to toil assiduously to make ends meet. To augment our meager resources, I used to tutor children in the neighborhood for peanuts. Things were gradually looking up, but I was thrifty with my salary.

"Are you going for the gala inauguration?" Lita asked casually while displaying her green ticket, which meant she had gotten a VIP ticket. Her dad was a big shot in the Agarwal company.

"No, I don't think I'll go; I'm not interested." Truth be told, I could not afford to spend one-tenth of my salary just to get a glimpse of RK. My kid brother Monty began to throw tantrums and pester me for money to buy a VIP ticket.

"Come on, sis, everyone is going, can't you spare a couple of bucks for me?" I was in a quandary. Should I waste so much money just so that Monty could keep up with the Joneses, vagabonds who did not do a stroke of work? I was torn between prudence and love for my brother. "If dad were alive, I'd never have to beg for these small favors," Monty said sullenly.

That did it. Monty was always a shrewd manipulator, and he got the better of me. I forked out a quarter of a month's salary to see the smile on my brother's face. Every day someone would come to the staff room flaunting and flashing the ticket. Rita's silver ticket got everyone's goat.

"I managed to get a silver," I told my dad. Yes, everyone knew her dad was the local politician. The color of the card indicated your status, gold being top-notch, and now the staff room was rented asunder by the color of the card, the complementary tickets, and tickets sold in black. The bragging went on, and I chose to maintain a discreet silence.

My small one BHK in Rohini Complex overlooked the large marquee, which was adjacent to the shopping arcade. So, I decided to just watch the show from my terrace. The day dawned bright and clear, and all roads seemed to lead to the Ram Swaroop Agarwal Market (RASAM). The acronym RASAM was appealing and delightful. However, the deafening cacophony of loudspeakers and never-ending "one, two, three, mike testing" gave me a severe headache.

Mother was at work and would not come before seven; Monty was already out of the house with the silver ticket, so I decided to rub some balm on my forehead and have a siesta. I shut the doors and windows to get some peace and quiet to do my correction and read the novel I had issued from the school library.

Unfortunately, I could not do any of those. The blaring music added to the raucous sound recorded the highest possible decibel, loud enough to wake up the dead. I lay on my bed, and I began to feel drowsy. The persistent ringing of the doorbell awakened me with a start. I glanced at the wall clock. It was only 11:30.

"Who's that?" I called out sleepily.

"Miss, it is me, Hema. Madam Paromita Mukherjee has sent me; please open the door." I was wide awake. Why would Pratima Mukherjee's maid come calling? I opened the door. Hema, the maid, gave me a note.

"Dear Glory teacher, I have two tickets for today's gala inauguration. Sir is unable to attend. Would you like to come with me? I can pick you up at 2:30. Paromita Mukherjee."

I stood there for what seemed like eternity. Mrs. Paromita Mukherjee was the high-profile wife of the

Director of Education. She had a sprawling bungalow about two hundred yards away from my down-market complex, and last year I taught her son Dhruv English and History. But to suddenly think of me and extend this fabulous invitation was unbelievable. My mind was in a tizzy. I hastily grabbed my pen and on the same paper, I simply wrote.

"Yes, thank you very much, Madam." I was thrilled to be invited to this grand show. Now I was flummoxed, not knowing what to wear; I hardly bought expensive sarees. I did have a vast collection of plain American georgettes and matched them with a couple of multicolored silk blouses.

"Calm down, Glory; it's only an inaugural function. Moreover, you are going to be a very unimportant guest, so just relax and take it easy." My inner voice always did the trick!! I felt like Cinderella, but where was my fairy godmother and the magic wand? I didn't even have a pumpkin Cinderella was better off. I smiled at my simile.

I opened my cupboard, pulled out my favorite green and gold chiffon saree. I kept reminding myself that nobody was going to give me even a side glance, so I needed to take it easy. Exactly at 2:30, the black

Mercedes Car drew up, and I could see my curious neighbor peeping indiscreetly. The liveried chauffeur opened the door for me, and I slid beside the petite Paromita Madam, the epitome of grace and charm.

After the initial pleasantries, she explained.

"I am so glad you came. In fact, Dhruv told me that you are staying so close, to invite you."

"I am also very happy to be invited, Madam," I said softly, filled with gratitude. We reached within minutes and were immediately escorted to the VVIP enclosure; so many dignitaries had already arrived. I could have been knocked down with a feather. Most of the special invitees were on a first-name basis with each other. The affable Paromita was clearly well-liked and admired.

I could see the marquee was packed to capacity. Mr. Ram Swaroop Agarwal was strutting back and forth with his minions in tow. Mrs. Agarwal, larger than life and laden with gold, was busy giving last-minute instructions.

But what unnerved me was the cold, hostile look I was given by the ushers. One Mr. Naresh even had the audacity to walk up to me and say, "Miss, you know these are VVIP seats. If you show me your ticket, I'll personally escort you to the correct seat." His patronizing tone added to my discomfiture.

"I have come with Paromita Madam." He looked at me in disbelief. How could I, a mere schoolteacher earning a three-figure salary, the daughter of a seamstress staying in one BHK, be rubbing shoulders with the who's who of the town?

I had prided myself once on my great literary skills, a topper in the university, ace debater, a prolific writer and an avid reader now struggling as a middle school teacher in a one-horse town. I had hopes of joining either the civil services or becoming a journalist, but my dad's death put an end to all my hopes and aspirations. I accepted my lot with equanimity, but on an occasion like this, I felt life did not play fair with me. The Naresh's of this world made it known to me that I was a misfit in this grand scheme of things, but the Paromita Mukherjee's of this world reinforced my faith in humanity.

The announcer's soft, lilting voice heralded the arrival of the great Raghav Kumar.

"On behalf of Ram Swaroop Agarwal and the RASAM fraternity, I heartily welcome the legend, the doyen of Indian Cinema, the one and only Raghav Kumar." The announcer went on to enumerate his many achievements, the accolades he had received and his "Hit" films, but all was lost on the thunderous applause that lasted a full five minutes. I could see the handsome hunk coming towards our row, and as if on cue, the five gentlemen sitting next to me all rose and vacated their seats, and Raghav Kumar and his entourage occupied those chairs.

The crowd cheered lustily as R.K. received his bouquets and gifts. Then Mr. Agarwal was requested, as per protocol, to escort Mr. Raghav Kumar to the podium where he released hundreds of multicolored balloons and declared the RASAM officially open.

Raghav Kumar came back to his seat next to mine; a battery of photographers began clicking, but he seemed engrossed in some conversation with Mr. Ashif Ali, who was an assistant director.

Then suddenly Raghav Kumar turned towards me; his million-dollar smile made me go weak in my knees.

"So, madam, what do you do...?" he asked cheerfully.

"Sir, I am a teacher... " I stuttered and stammered and took forever to reply.

"Teacher, good. I am sure your students love you. My dad was a teacher and taught Chemistry in Government School. But I was the black sheep of the family. I wanted to become an actor, so I dropped out after Class X. I preferred acting." He said this softly as if talking to himself. In between, he was besieged with fans with autographs, and he graciously obliged.

Then he said with all the histrionics at his command, "You know, you will always be remembered by your students. Our fame and glory are transitory." I listened in rapt attention as RK spoke to me about the highs and lows of his professions. I knew I was the cynosure of all eyes, I wanted to hold on to this moment forever. I was living a dream."

Raghav Kumar suddenly stood up, his bodyguard rushed towards him, and in a flash, he exited, slipped out quietly without much ado. I felt empty and sad. This is how Cinderella must have felt when she had to leave the prince at the stroke of midnight.

The next day's newspapers all had Raghav Kumar and Me on the front page. I smiled as I recalled the famous Poet Byron's words:

"I woke up one morning and found myself famous."

Closure

Kannama threw up her bony hands and smiled incredulously, "Oh madam, you really had a wonderful experience as a teacher, didn't you?" Then Kannama narrowed her eyes and whispered in a conspiratorial voice, "But what about the boy, the guards keep talking about it."

Kannama, sly horse wanted to elicit some information about the case that rocked the town and sent shock waves across the city about twenty years ago, but like ghost stories, these stories too were passed down by word of mouth and refused to completely die down. But Miss Molly was in no mood to oblige the inquisitive maid, nevertheless, this jogged her memory, and she literally took a walk down memory lane.

"Make me some nice hot coffee, Kanni," she ordered, then reclined in her easy chair and closed her eyes and drifted into a summer slumber. The fragrance of the flowers in her small garden and the aroma of the coffee lulled her senses, and she went back in time.

"Madam, may I come in?" Molly looked up to see a gaunt, emaciated teenager with disheveled hair standing in front of her. "Yes, come in. You are Sourav Tiwary – Class XI science." She knew him well but feigned ignorance. Two days earlier his father, Inspector Shambhunath Tiwary, had paid her a sudden unexpected visit. Of course, she was getting used to his intrusion in her spare time. Miss Molly was a middle school teacher at Central High Residential School, but since late she has been given additional responsibility of overseeing the Boarder's homework and general discipline in the hostel. She soon gained the confidence of the defiant, senior students and being good in English, she spent her spare time helping the seniors in language and literature. Miss Molly, a spinster, was given a room in the school premises, with an adjoining office to meet parents and guardians.

So today, in spite of her severe migraine, she warmly welcomed this tall, strapping man in uniform. "I have come to discuss Saurav my son, Madam." "I am sorry I have come without prior appointment, but our..." He tried to justify his visit. "It's okay, Mr. Tiwary. You may speak out," she urged him after seeing his hesitation and discomfort. "Saurav was a topper in school, now he has deteriorated to the extent that he may fail this year." Mr. Tiwary went on to explain why he put his son Saurav in a hostel. His son lacked guidance and was always seen in the company of loafers and "third-rate scoundrels." Tiwary spoke about how his subordinates passed sly innuendoes about officers who are so busy apprehending criminals that they do not know what is happening in their own lives. Now, Inspector Tiwary whipped out a large handkerchief and blew his nose noisily and wiped his face vigorously. Molly ordered some coffee for the guest, which he slurped and spilled a lot.

Tiwary concluded his dramatic monologue. He requested Miss Molly to please talk to his son. "Mr. Tiwary, I made a note of what you said. I shall talk to Saurav at the earliest."

Now today this young boy was facing her—a chip of the old block, she thought. "Good evening son." Molly had realized long ago that if she addressed the boy as 'son,' a bond was created, 'son' or 'beta' worked like abracadabra. "So, beta, how are you doing? I did not get to see your last report card," she said gently. "Miss, I did not do too well." He was squirming in his seat and fidgeting more than necessary. But what unnerved Miss Molly was his blank, vacant look, which sent a shiver down her spine. "Did you watch the cricket match yesterday – Red House versus Green House? It was so exciting." She tried to change tack but drew a blank. "No, I was sleeping. Not interested in cricket." He averted her gaze. Now Miss Molly tried to engage him in a conversation on a gamut of topics, but he was a tough nut to crack. Molly too was made of sterner stuff, and she knew beneath his impenetrable veneer, there was a small, vulnerable child in need of love and compassion.

Then she went for the jugular. "Look Sourav, you may not be allowed to answer your boards next year in March, as your attendance too is quite poor, and your marks are even worse, so you will be struck off the rolls. Even in your class X Boards, you barely scraped by the skin of your teeth. So could you please tell me what is happening?" She raised her voice enough to cause alarm. "Miss, it is a long story, I want to tell you everything. It is a sordid saga; I want to come clean. But please, miss, do not tell my father anything." He spoke, his voice was quivering. But, in spite of his impressive vocabulary, Molly was sitting on a razor's edge. There was something sinister about this boy's demeanor, his ingratiating smile troubled her, but she was still in command.

She was clearly straddling two worlds: one with a deceitful sly child, and the other with a small, motherless boy and a larger-than-life, unsympathetic father. "Oh yes, sure, let me check my diary." She was clearly buying time. "How about Thursday, prep time?" Miss Molly smiled cheerfully; glad this meeting was coming to an end. Saurav rose and came forward to touch her feet, but even this nice gesture scared her today.

That night, two people had weight lifted from their shoulders. Miss Molly felt relieved the worst was over, and Sourav felt a new chapter in his life had begun. The next two days were bliss, Sourav's friends were amazed at his newfound exuberance and neat and clean-shaven appearance. He even appreciated the bland and insipid hostel food. He joined his friends for a game of chess in the common room. Miss Molly, in the meanwhile, had got back to her mundane routine duties. Though she was tired, she was thankful that she did not have to cook or clean and do any household chores. The hostel food was nutritious, and the cleaners were honest. This suited her fine. The shrill ring of the telephone shattered the tranquility of the night. Who could this late caller be? It was Julie, Molly's sister from Ramnagar.

"Hello Molly" then, Julie informed Molly of her octogenarian mother's fall in the washroom, hospitalization, and the surgery scheduled for Thursday morning – It was a femur fracture. The next day, Wednesday, after school hours, Molly rushed to the bus stand and reached home around six thirty. "Where is my mother? Let's go and see her." Molly and her sister jumped into a cab and reached the hospital. After checking with the doctors, Molly made a phone call to the school Principal Miss Zarine Billimoria, who immediately sanctioned the leave telephonically. So, Molly was at ease, but she had to get around getting things organized. Thursday was a hectic day: rushing to the bank, blood bank, every detail to be seen. The surgery was successful, and Dr. Pranab Bose smiled gleefully. Then he rattled off some do's and don'ts. The D'sas enjoyed a hearty meal in the hospital cafeteria and discussed some inconsequential family matters.

On Sunday, Miss Molly wished and kissed her mother and then hailed a cab. The bus journey was uneventful, and the bus was packed to capacity with locals carrying their wares. She reached her hostel well past dinner time. So she unpacked her bag and ate the leathery parathas and pungent potato curry. Thank God, Julie had packed some Indian sweets. Molly was lost in thought, thinking of her mother, Julie, the expenses incurred during this hospitalization. But in spite of her fatigue, she could sense rather than see movement near the hostel, was it an optical illusion or were the men really the police in uniform. Perhaps some new admission, army or police personnel's ward. Monday morning was business as usual for Miss D'Sa, but the posse of policemen were still loitering around the hostel premises.

Her heart skipped a beat. The Chairman and the Principal were with the police. She walked gingerly towards them, "Ah here's Miss D'Sa, the Hostel co-coordinator," Mrs. Billmoria said by way of introduction. Then she almost retched when she saw Mr. Shambhunath Tiwary, eyes swollen, bloodshot, in civilian clothes." It's Saurav Tiwary, Miss D'Sa. He is no more." What a euphemism for death! "Oh no, no, no, Ma'am how? When?" She stifled a sob. Mr. Tiwary looked past her, in fact, he looked at her and then looked through her, a look she will never forget. Then Mr. Sameer Sen, the garrulous Estate Officer started blabbering incoherently about suicide hanging from the ceiling fan. "Oh my God, I wish he would stop." But he went on and on. He was telling other boys that someone was supposed to meet him, but he let him down. The needle of suspicion would point towards Molly.

"What exactly happened, Samir?" she asked when she moved away from the Chairman and the Principal. "I really don't know, but boys were telling me he was crying the whole Friday morning and evening, he kept saying somebody was to meet him but did not come." Samir with his broken English, conveyed a very scary message. "He was crying and he was let down." But Sameer the quintessential old-timer reckoned it was unrequited love that drove this boy to suicide in the dilapidated building. Miss Molly's head was spinning with fear, anxiety and sorrow. The news of this tragedy spread like wildfire, and the agitated parents demanded strict action against all those who aided and abetted the suicide. Some parents even wrote letters withdrawing their children from the hostel.

The Managing Committee convened an emergent meeting to discuss the fallout of this unfortunate incident. The school held an all-faith prayer meeting. The Board also advised Mrs. Billmorea to bring forward the Class IX-XII exams to keep the students busy and not indulge in "Loose talk." Conspiracy theories were flying thick and fast, and it was encumbered upon the principal and staff to preempt any effort to malign the institution. Miss Molly became subdued and withdrawn, wracked as she was with guilt and remorse. "She cried every night for the loss of a life." Five years later, an ex-student Arnab Mitra dropped in to pay her a visit. This was common especially in residential schools, students came back, especially if they had migrated, to relive old memories of days gone by. The naughtier the student, the stronger the bond with the alma mater.

So, after the initial small talk about his master's degree at Michigan University and his desire to serve his motherland, he dropped the bombshell. "You know, teacher, I still remember my best friend Sourav, you know, Saurav Tiwary?" Molly prayed for an earthquake. Why is this boy raking up old issues? She waved her hand dismissively and said, "Oh, that old story." But her heart was beating violently. "I had promised to meet him at the hostel gate on Friday evening after dinner that fateful day. He wanted to tell me about someone who was blackmailing him. He was petrified. He couldn't confide in his dad, whom he dreaded and his mother whom he detested, and a sister who shunned him. This was a truly dysfunctional family teacher. But I could not meet him because I did not want to get involved in his personal matters and at the last minute, I got cold feet." "Teacher, I'm filled with guilt." "It is okay, son." She commiserated with him and then said inaudibly, "That makes two of us."

When Arnab bid her goodbye, Molly felt the Sword of Democeles had been lifted. All along she had believed she was responsible for Saurab's death and now it was time to move on. "Madam, your coffee is getting cold." Kannama whispered softly. But Molly was fast asleep.

www.ingramcontent.com/pod-product-compliance
Lightning Source LLC
LaVergne TN
LVHW061602070526
838199LV00077B/7149